POKÉMON
BLACK & WHITE

SANDILE IN TROUBLE

Based on the episode *"Dancing With the Ducklett Trio!"*

by Simcha Whitehill

ISBN 978-0-545-38072-0

© 2012 Pokémon. ©1997-2012 Nintendo, Creatures, GAME FREAK, TV Tokyo, ShoPro, JR Kikaku. TM, ® Nintendo. All rights reserved.
Published by Scholastic Inc.
SCHOLASTIC and associated logos are trademarks and/or registered trademarks of Scholastic Inc.

12 11 10 9 8 7 6 5 4 3 2 1   12 13 14 15 16 17/0

Designed by Henry Ng
Printed in the U.S.A.   40
First printing, January 2012

New York   Auckland
Sydney   Hong Kong

Ash, Cilan, and Iris were taking a break outside Castelia City. While Cilan made lunch, Ash and Iris decided to give Scraggy and Axew a little practice.

"*Scraggy!*" the little Dark- and Fighting-type cried.

"*Axew, ax!*" Axew cheered.

The practice battle began.

"Okay, Axew, Dragon Rage, let's go!" Iris said.

But Axew couldn't control the attack. Dragon Rage blew up into the sky like fireworks.

"Well, we tried!" Iris laughed.

"Hey, gang! Lunch is all ready!"
Cilan called.

As he lifted the cover from the
food, a Ducklett swooped in and
stole the silver top!

"Ha, ha, ha!" the Ducklett laughed
as it ran off.

Then something even stranger happened! The ground beneath Ash and Pikachu started to move. Suddenly, the Trainer and his best pal were falling through a long, dark tunnel.

"*Whoooooa!*" Ash yelled as he slid down, down, down.

Ash and Pikachu landed at the bottom of a mountain. A Sandile wearing sunglasses greeted them. But it wasn't just any Sandile. . . .

"Hey, aren't you the Sandile we battled back at the Hot Sands Spa?" Ash asked.

"*Sandile, sand,*" it said, nodding. Sandile had brought Ash and Pikachu to the bottom of the mountain for a rematch!

"What do you say, Pikachu?" Ash asked his Pokémon.

"*Pika, pika!*" Pikachu cheered.

Just then, a Ducklett wandered onto the middle of the field.

"We're kind of in the middle of a battle. Would you mind moving to the sidelines?" Ash asked.

Ducklett refused to move. So Sandile nudged it with its nose.

Ducklett tickled Sandile's nose with the feathers on its wings.

"*Achooooooo!*" Sandile sneezed so hard, its sunglasses flew off its face. Ducklett grabbed the sunglasses and put them on.

"*Sand, sandile.*" Sandile asked for its favorite pair of shades back. Ducklett took them off. But instead of handing them back, Ducklett blasted Sandile with Water Gun!

"Ha, ha, ha!" Ducklett laughed. It flew away with Sandile's sunglasses.

Sandile was sad. It really loved those sunglasses.

"Don't worry, Sandile! I'll get your glasses back!" Ash promised.

"*Pika!*" Pikachu agreed.

"*Sandile, sand,*" Sandile thanked them. It was happy to have friends to help.

Just then, another Ducklett
swooped in. It snatched Ash's hat.
"Hey, give that back!" Ash yelled.
Ducklett didn't like being shouted
at. It shot Ice Beam at Ash.
Ash dodged Ducklett's attack. But
the Water- and Flying-type still flew
off with his cap.

Ash, Pikachu, and Sandile chased after Ducklett. It led them to a riverbank, where it joined the Ducklett that had stolen Cilan's cover and the Ducklett that had stolen Sandile's sunglasses.

"Now we've got to deal with three of them!" Ash cried.

Ash was fed up. He was ready
to battle. But three Ducklett
versus Pikachu and Sandile
wasn't a fair fight.

"Ha, ha, ha!" the Ducklett
laughed at them.

"Pikachu, use Thunderbolt!"
Ash cried.

"*Pikaaaachuuuuu!*" Pikachu
yelled, zapping the Ducklett.

But one of the Ducklett was
able to dodge the attack. It flew
right into Pikachu and Sandile
with Wing Attack.

One Ducklett splashed Ash with
Scald. Then another trapped Ash in
Ice Beam.

"Man, that's cold!" Ash shivered
from inside a big block of ice.

Sandile bit through the giant ice cube and freed Ash.

"Hey, Sandile . . . thanks!" Ash said.

Meanwhile, the Ducklett had flown into a tree house. Ash, Pikachu, and Sandile ran after them.

The Ducklett threw stuff at them—
a soccer ball, a broken chair, a red
guitar, a pink umbrella. Pikachu tried
to unleash Thunderbolt, but it got
trapped inside the umbrella.

"*Pikkkaaaaaaaaa!*" Pikachu
yelped. It was caught in its own
Electric-type attack!

Ash and Sandile risked getting zapped to pull Pikachu out of the pink umbrella.

"Pikachu, are you okay?" Ash asked.

"*Piiiiikaaa,*" it sighed as it shed extra electricity.

Suddenly, the Ducklett swooped back in, shooting Scald.

"Come on, let's get out of here!" Ash yelled to Sandile.

"Ha, ha, ha!" the Ducklett laughed.

Ash and his friends hid and spied on the Ducklett. "Man, look at all the stuff they've got," Ash sighed.

Ash, Pikachu, and Sandile were outnumbered. So Ash came up with a new plan. He walked right up to the Ducklett.

"We don't want to fight you. We just want our stuff back," Ash explained.

It seemed like the Ducklett were
moved by Ash's speech.

One Ducklett slowly walked over to
Ash, Pikachu, and Sandile. It held out
the sunglasses.

"Wow! You're going to give them
back?" Ash said.

But when it got close, Ducklett surprised them with Water Gun.

"Ha, ha, ha!" the Ducklett all laughed.

There was only one thing to do: stand up to these bullies!

"Pikachu, use Thunderbolt now!" Ash yelled.

But Pikachu's Electric-type attacks weren't working right. So Sandile stepped in.

"*Sandile!*" it said. It wasn't afraid of Ducklett anymore. Now it was all fired up!

"We're here if you need us, okay?" said Ash.

It was three against one! Plus, Ducklett's Water-type attacks were very powerful against a Ground-type like Sandile.

But Sandile had smarts on its side. It started with Stone Edge, a Rock-type move that was very effective against Ducklett.

One Ducklett fired back with Ice
Beam. Another Ducklett shot Scald.
And the third one used Water Gun.
"Dodge them, Sandile!" Ash cried.

Sandile was in trouble. The three Ducklett were overpowering it. So Pikachu stepped in with Iron Tail to help block the attacks.

But the Ducklett trio zoomed at them. They knocked Ash, Sandile, and Pikachu around with Wing Attack.

Suddenly, Pikachu blasted the Ducklett away with an incredible Electro Ball.

"Whoa, Pikachu!" Ash said. He was amazed by his Pokémon's powerful new move.

Pikachu's Electro Ball was so bright that Cilan, Iris, and Axew were finally able to find their friends in the forest. Ash quickly told them everything that had happened with the Ducklett. "You mean there are actually three Ducklett?" Cilan asked.

Just then, the three Ducklett
swooped back in. They spurted
Scald at the three friends.

"What's wrong with you guys?"
Iris cried.

"Such behavior is hard to
understand," Cilan said.

Ash and Pikachu had had it. "Pikachu! Use Thunderbolt!" Ash cried.

"*Pikachuuuu!*" yelped Pikachu, firing the attack.

That scared the Ducklett off for good!

"Way to go, Pikachu!" Ash cheered.

Sandile thanked Ash and Pikachu for their help. "*Sandile, sand.*"

"Well, those Ducklett caused a lot of trouble, but because of them, Pikachu learned a brand-new move! Right, buddy?" said Ash.

"*Pika, pika!*" Pikachu agreed. It was ready for its next adventure in Unova.